SUPER SPIES OF WORLD WAR II

SPIES AND SPYING

KATE **WALKER** I ELAINE **ARGAET**

This edition first published in 2004 in the United States of America by Smart Apple Media.

Smart Apple Media
1980 Lookout Drive
North Mankato
Minnesota 56003

Library of Congress Cataloging-in-Publication Data

Walker, Kate.
   Super spies of World War II / by Kate Walker & Elaine Argaet.
   p. cm. — (Spies and spying)

   Includes index.
   Contents: Nancy Wake, the White Mouse—Wilhelm Canaris, the German spy who hated Hitler—Amelia Earhart, the spy over the Pacific—Eddie Chapman, safe breaker and spy—Witold Pilecki, the death camp spy—Noor Inayat Khan, the princess spy—Takeo Yoshikawa, Japan's Pearl Harbor spy—Elyesa Bazna, code name Cicero— Mathilde Carré, the spy who turned traitor—Donald Kennedy, the coast watcher—Chistine Granville, beauty queen and spy—Ted Hall, the boy who gave away the atom bomb—Hans and Sophie Scholl, and the White Rose.

   ISBN 1-58340-340-X
   1. Spies—History—20th century—Juvenile literature. 2. World War, 1939–1945—Secret service—Juvenile literature. [1. Espionage—History—20th century. 2. Spies. 3. World War, 1939–1945—Secret service.] I. Argaet, Elaine. II. Title. III. Series.
   D810.S7W34 2003
   940.54'85'0922—dc
   [B]   200204462021

First Edition
9 8 7 6 5 4 3 2 1

First published in 2003 by
MACMILLAN EDUCATION AUSTRALIA PTY LTD
627 Chapel Street, South Yarra, Australia, 3141

Associated companies and representatives throughout the world.

Edited by Miriana Dasovic
Text and cover design by Marta White
Maps by Pat Kermode, Purple Rabbit Productions
Photo research by Jes Senbergs

Printed in Thailand

Acknowledgements

The author and the publisher are grateful to the following for permission to reproduce copyright material:

Cover photograph: Amelia Earhart, and magnifying glass, courtesy of Getty Images; eye, courtesy of Ingram Royalty Free Image Library.

AAP/AFP Photo, p. 29 (center); Archiv Gerstenberg, p. 30; Australian Picture Library/Corbis, pp. 4 (bottom), 19, 21, 27; Australian War Memorial negative number 306807, p. 25 (top); Australian War Memorial negative number 306809, p. 25 (bottom); Australian War Memorial negative number p00885001, p. 7 (top); © Bildarchiv Preussischer Kulturbeitz, Berlin, p. 8; Cooee Historical Picture Library, p. 11 (top); Getty Images, pp. 1, 3, 9, 11 (bottom), 15 (bottom), 23 (top), 32 (all); Ingram Royalty Free Image Library, pp. 1 (eye), 20 (right); Theodore Hall, p. 28, in *Bombshell* by J. Albright and M. Kunstel, Time Books, Random House, NY, 1997; The Director, National Army Museum, London, p. 7 (bottom); Picture Post, p. 26, in *Spies and Traitors*, by Kurt Singer, WH Allen, London, 1953, p. 160; Hart Preston for *Life*, Durriye Bazna, Munich, p. 20 (left), in *World War II – The Secret War*, edited by Francis Russell, Time-Life Books, Chicago, 1981; The Public Record Office, p. 13 ; Roger Viollet, p. 23 (bottom); photo p. 18 from *Spies, A Narrative Encyclopedia*, by J. Robert Nash, M. Evans & Com Inc, NY, 1997; The State Museum of Auschwitz-Birkenau, p. 15 (top); The Trustees of the Imperial War Museum, London, pp. 4 (top), 16, 17.

While every care has been taken to trace and acknowledge copyright, the publisher tenders their apologies for any accidental infringement where copyright has proved untraceable. Where the attempt has been unsuccessful, the publisher welcomes information that would redress the situation.

CONTENTS

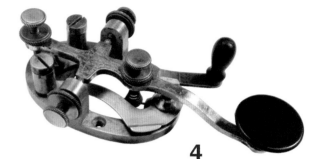

INTRODUCTION

An agent on the side of Britain, Belgium, and France uses a radio transmitter in the field.

British soldiers at a checkpoint in Germany check a German man's **identity card**. Spies had false identity cards and passes so they could move from town to town.

What is a spy?

A spy is a person who deals in secret information. Some spies gather the information, usually by sly means. Other spies carry the information from one person to another. There are spies who sit at desks and study the information, while other spies go out into the field and act on it. Some spies make up false information and spread it around to fool the enemy. Anyone who works secretly in this way is a spy.

- 👁 The proper name for spying is espionage.
- 👁 The modern name for a spy is an agent or intelligence officer.
- 👁 Information gathered by spies is called intelligence.

When did spying start?

People have been spying on each other since human history began. Army leaders have always known that the best way to defeat an enemy is to find out that enemy's weakness, and the best person to discover that weakness is a spy.

Why do people become spies?

Sometimes people become spies out of loyalty to their country. They gather information that will help keep their country safe. Sometimes people become spies because they know important secret information and sell it for money, usually a lot of money. Some people are tricked or forced into becoming spies. Other people choose to become spies because they find it exciting.

Germany begins the war

World War II began on September 3, 1939, when Germany invaded Poland. Germany was led by Adolf Hitler and his Nazi Party, and they planned to take over the whole of Europe. Japan became an ally of Germany. Japan was also planning to take over other countries. It was led by Emperor Hirohito, who wanted to make Japan ruler of Asia and the South Pacific.

Allies | Axis powers | Neutral countries

Training the spies

When war broke out, thousands of spies were recruited by both sides. Special schools and training camps were set up to teach spies different skills. Spies learned to use complicated codes for sending radio messages. Civilian spies were trained to use weapons and to fight. Spies who were already members of the armed forces were given extra training in deadly fighting skills. They also learned to build and lay bombs.

Britain relies on its spies

Britain and its allies did not have strong armies. They seemed to have very little chance of winning the war. This forced them to use spies and clever tricks as never before. Spies in World War II did more than gather information. They actively engaged in fighting as secret warriors. This meant that spying had become more dangerous than ever before.

World War II ended in Europe when Germany surrendered on May 8, 1945, and ended in the Pacific when Japan surrendered on August 14 that year.

ally   a country that helps and supports another country

civilian   a person not in the armed forces

codes   secret languages

identity card   an official card with a person's name and photograph that proves who they are

into the field   going into other countries to spy

Nazi Party   a brutal political and military group that governed Germany from 1933 to 1949

recruited   asked to do a job

NANCY WAKE, THE WHITE MOUSE

Nancy Wake: 1912–
Born: Wellington, New Zealand
Spied for Britain and France against Germany

Helping a stranded pilot

Nancy Wake was living in France when the German army invaded. One day, she and her husband were in a café in Paris when they saw a young man reading an English book. Wake spoke to him. He was an English pilot who had been shot down and needed help to get out of France. Wake and her husband drove the young man south. There were German soldiers everywhere, but the Wakes managed to smuggle the young pilot across the border safely into neutral Spain. From Spain he could make his way back to England.

Setting up an escape route

Wake decided that she must help other stranded soldiers. She bought an ambulance. Over the next few months, she drove this vehicle back and forth between France and the border of Spain. She hid Allied soldiers and pilots in the back, and helped them reach the border. There they could dash across to safety. This escape route was called a "rat line." After a while, the Germans became suspicious of Wake's movements. She was finally forced to flee France herself.

N

BRITAIN
ENGLAND
GERMANY
• Paris
Belfort •
FRANCE
Auvergne
SPAIN

0   300 miles

Wake returns to France as a fighter

Wake was determined to keep on helping the French in their fight against the Germans. In Britain, she trained as a fighter and slipped secretly back into France again. Her job was to contact the many small Resistance groups in the Auvergne district and turn them into one strong fighting force. The British dropped boxes of weapons by parachute at night. Wake's Resistance group collected these weapons and hid them in secret stores. Wake then handed out these weapons to any other group that would fight with hers.

The White Mouse

Wake's Auvergne Resistance fighters began attacking German convoys of soldiers and supplies. The Germans soon realized that someone new was running the Resistance in Auvergne. They called this person the White Mouse, although they did not know who it was.

Wake was often right under their noses. One time, she cycled 310 miles (500 km) through several German checkpoints to deliver a radio. Another time, she sneaked through the forest of Terre de Belfort and blew up the bridges across the river near Belfort. This left a large number of German soldiers stranded. Allied forces soon overtook them and they were forced to surrender.

A sad end

The war ended in 1945. Wake drove to Paris to celebrate. There she learned that her husband had been caught by the Germans. He had been shot because he refused to tell them what he knew about the White Mouse.

Nancy Wake.

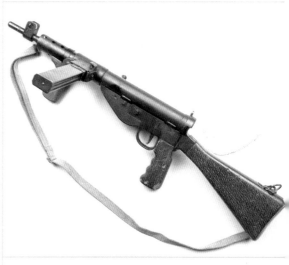

The Sten gun was a lightweight weapon used by French Resistance fighters.

Allied soldiers   soldiers fighting on the side of the Allies (Britain, Belgium, and France)

convoys   lines of vehicles

invaded   used military force to enter someone else's land

neutral   not taking one side or the other in a fight

WILHELM CANARIS, THE GERMAN SPY WHO HATED HITLER

BACKGROUND

- Adolf Hitler and his Nazis planned to murder all the people they did not like.

- Many German people disagreed with Hitler and wanted to stop him.

Admiral Wilhelm Canaris, head of the German secret service.

Wilhelm Canaris: 1887–1945
Born: Dortmund, Germany
Spied for Germany against the Allies

Halfway around the world

Wilhelm Canaris was a young naval cadet in World War I. When his ship was sunk off the coast of Chile, Canaris swam ashore. He trekked hundreds of miles over the Chilean mountains and down into Argentina. There he used a false name and managed to get a passport. He boarded a Dutch ship and sailed safely home to Germany. Because of his courage, the navy decided that Canaris should be trained as a spy.

Escape artist

On his first mission, Canaris went to Spain and set up secret bases for German submarines. One night, he was spotted by enemy agents. He jumped into a small boat and sailed far out into the Mediterranean Sea. A German submarine surfaced, picked him up, and whisked him away. His next close call came in Italy, when he was stopped by border police. They suspected him of spying and put him in a prison cell. Canaris asked to see a priest. A few hours later, Canaris escaped wearing the priest's clothes.

Canaris sets up a spy screen

When World War II started in 1939, Canaris was made chief of the German secret service. He sent hundreds of spies into Britain. Most of them were untrained, so they were asked to simply listen for any information that might help Germany. Canaris said that this large number of minor (unimportant) spies formed a screen that hid the few important spies he sent. Most of these minor spies were Jewish women who went to work in wealthy English homes. Very few of these women spoke English. At that time, Jewish people in Germany were being herded into prison camps by the Nazis. By sending them to Britain, Canaris helped them escape from the Nazis.

Losing the war for his country

Canaris loved his country, but he believed that Hitler was a madman and had to be stopped. So Canaris sneaked information to the Allies about German military plans. He believed that the best thing he could do for his country was to help it lose the war. Other Germans felt the same.

The bomb plot

In July 1944, a group of German military officers planted a bomb in a hall where Hitler was supposed to give a speech. The bomb went off before Hitler arrived. Hitler was so angry that he had hundreds of German officers arrested. Canaris was one of them. Hitler learned that Canaris had known about the plot but had done nothing to stop it. Canaris was executed and his secret service was closed down.

Some poor Jewish women were sent to England by Canaris to work as spies. Most, however, were forced into prison camps by the Nazis.

passport an official identification document needed by someone traveling to another country

secret service another name for a spy network

AMELIA EARHART, THE SPY OVER THE PACIFIC

BACKGROUND

At the beginning of World War II, Japan had troops on many small islands in the Pacific Ocean.

Japanese patrol boats would not let anyone near these islands.

Amelia Earhart: 1897–1937
Born: Kansas, United States
Spied for the U.S. against Japan

Earhart crashes in a cabbage patch

Amelia Earhart was 23 years old when she took her first flight. She loved it and knew immediately she wanted to be a pilot. A year later, she had gained a pilot's license and bought her own plane. Earhart had a serious crash when her plane came down in a cabbage patch. She said that the accident soured her on cabbages but not on flying.

The first woman ever

In 1932, Earhart was the first woman to fly across the Atlantic Ocean. Three years later, she became the first woman to fly across the Pacific Ocean. Earhart began to make plans to become the first woman to fly right around the world.

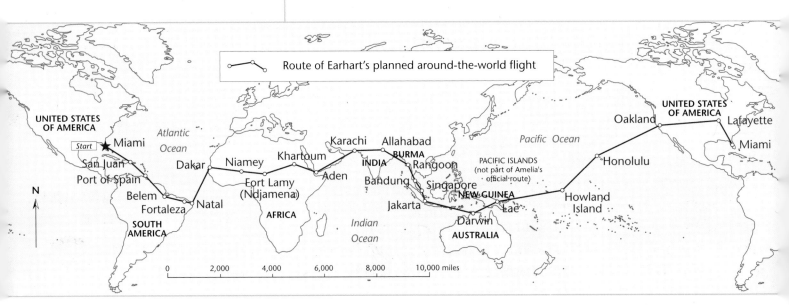

Route of Earhart's planned around-the-world flight

Famous flight or secret spy mission?

On June 1, 1937, Earhart took off from Miami, Florida. This was the beginning of her around-the-world flight. Part of this flight would take her over the Pacific Islands, held by the Japanese. The U.S. navy had been trying to get a look at these islands for a long time. The navy was sure that the Japanese were building secret naval bases there.

A dot in the ocean

The most difficult part of Earhart's journey was the long stretch across the Pacific Ocean. She needed to stop somewhere along the way to take on more fuel. Tiny Howland Island was chosen as her refueling stop. This island was less than 2 miles (3 km) long and one-third of a mile (0.5 km) wide.

The plane never arrives

Earhart's last radio message was heard when she was 99 miles (160 km) from Howland Island. She never landed, and no more radio calls were heard from her. The U.S. navy searched the ocean for her, but found nothing. It is now believed that Earhart agreed to fly over the islands where the Japanese were secretly building naval wharves. Earhart had a navigator with her, Fred Noonan. He had spied for the navy before and would know what to look for.

Rumors

After the war, local people on an island near Howland told a strange story. They said that a white woman and a white man had been held as prisoners of the Japanese. No one knows if this story is true. Earhart disappeared without a trace. If she had been shot down, the Japanese would have been careful to destroy every single piece of her plane.

Amelia Earhart in her flying gear.

Amelia Earhart at the controls of her plane.

license   a document showing that a person has been given permission to do a special task or job

navigator   a person who works out which direction to go

refueling stop   a place to fill up with more fuel

EDDIE CHAPMAN, SAFE-BREAKER AND SPY

Eddie Chapman: 1914–97
Born: Tyne, England
Spied for Britain against Germany

BACKGROUND

German forces landed on the Channel Islands in June 1942.

The Channel Islands are part of Britain.

Master thief

Eddie Chapman was an English safe-breaker. He opened safes by cracking their codes or by using explosives to blow them up. He stole large amounts of money and jewels. British police finally caught him, and he was sent to prison on the Channel Islands. When the Germans invaded the Channel Islands, they found Chapman pacing in his cell. He told them he hated the British and would happily spy against them.

Put to the test

The Germans were not sure if Chapman was telling the truth. As a test, they asked him to blow up the de Havilland aircraft factory in Hatfield. Chapman said he would blow it sky high! On December 20, 1942, he parachuted from a German plane and landed safely in an English field. Chapman walked to the nearest railroad station and caught a train to London. Over the next few weeks, he sent coded messages to his German spy chiefs. In one message, he told them he had the explosives for the job. On January 29, 1943, he sent a message to say that the de Havilland factory would "go up" at six o'clock that night.

N

BRITAIN

Tyne

ENGLAND
Hatfield
London

GERMANY

Channel Islands

0   300 miles

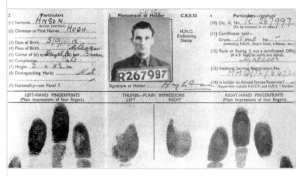

Eddie Chapman's false identity card, showing the name Hugh Anson.

The proof

The next day, German planes flew over the de Havilland factory and took photographs that showed wide holes in the roof. Broken machinery was scattered across the ground. The factory looked thoroughly wrecked. From that day, the Germans trusted Chapman. He stayed in England and sent information to the Germans about British and Allied troops. Most of this information was false. Eddie Chapman was actually a double agent. While pretending to spy for the Germans, he was really helping the British.

What really happened to the factory?

When Chapman arrived in London, he had gone straight to British intelligence. He told the intelligence officers about his job to blow up the factory, and they came up with a clever idea. They pulled large pieces of canvas over the factory roof, and painted pictures on the canvas that looked like holes with wreckage strewn below. Papier-mâché models were made of parts of the factory's machinery. These fake parts were scattered on the ground. Piles of bricks and smashed furniture were added to the mess. To check that the wreckage looked real, British planes had flown over and taken pictures of it.

Fake damage painted onto and scattered around the de Havilland aircraft factory in Hatfield.

No longer a criminal

When the war ended in 1945, Eddie Chapman was made a free man. For helping his country win the war, his criminal record was destroyed.

double agent   a spy pretending to work for one country while secretly working for another

papier-mâché   wet paper and paste that is molded into shape and dries hard

WITOLD PILECKI, THE DEATH-CAMP SPY

Witold Pilecki: 1901–48
Born: Poland
Spied for Poland against Germany

BACKGROUND

- Germany invaded Poland in 1939 and defeated it quickly.

- The Germans put Polish soldiers into prison camps.

- They also arrested ordinary Polish people and sent them to prison camps.

The prison camps

Witold Pilecki was a captain in the Polish army when his country was defeated by Germany. Pilecki could have escaped, but he chose to stay and keep on fighting. He joined the Polish Underground army in Warsaw. Pilecki did not like the terrible stories he heard about the prison camps. He asked his commanding officer for permission to try to get into one of the camps and find out if the reports were true. Pilecki also hoped to lead a mass break-out of prisoners.

Getting into a camp

Pilecki got a forged identity card in the name of Tomasz Serafinski. It was a very poor forgery, and he was arrested by the first German soldier who stopped him to check his card. Pilecki was sent to a camp at Auschwitz. He soon learned that all the terrible stories he had heard were true. In the camp, the guards treated the prisoners very badly. Prisoners were often beaten, and sometimes shot for no reason. The Germans made the prisoners work long hours building new huts. Clearly the Germans planned to imprison more people.

Getting messages out

Pilecki found a way of getting reports out of the camp. Some prisoners carved wooden statues to sell in a local village market.

Witold Pilecki, also known as Tomasz Serafinski, prisoner number 4859.

Pilecki got the carvers to make some of the statues hollow, and he hid his reports inside. These statues were secretly sent to officers of the Underground.

Three years in Auschwitz

Pilecki organized the Auschwitz prisoners into small groups that could help one another. His most important group worked in the camp hospital. German guards were afraid to come near the hospital in case they caught a disease. Pilecki was able to hide things in the hospital. He also held meetings and made plans. By 1942, he had a group of 500 prisoners ready to try to break out. First, Pilecki had to get weapons for them.

The entrance to the Auschwitz labor camp was known as the Gate of Death.

Escape

Pilecki used a homemade key to open the back door of the camp bakery and get away under cover of night. He crept down to a nearby river, only to find that the water was flowing too fast for him to swim across. There was a boat on the riverbank, but it was chained to a tree with a padlock. Pilecki tried the bakery key in the padlock. To his surprise, it opened. Pilecki got back to Warsaw and told the Underground of his plans for the break-out. The Underground could not help him because there were no weapons to spare. Pilecki had done all he could to help the Auschwitz prisoners. He spent the rest of the war as a soldier with the Underground army.

NOOR INAYAT KHAN, THE PRINCESS SPY

Noor Inayat Khan: 1914–44
Born: Moscow, Russia (of an Indian father)
Spied for Britain and France against Germany

The Princess volunteers to spy

Noor Inayat Khan was an Indian princess who was living in France when the German army invaded. She escaped to England, but soon volunteered to return to France and work as a spy. She trained as a radio operator, and learned the special radio codes quickly. However, her teachers thought she would make a terrible spy. Inayat Khan had been raised in the Sufi religion, and refused to ever tell a lie.

The clothesline

In June 1943, Inayat Khan arrived back in France. Her job was to collect information from other spies and radio it to Britain in secret code. She rented a room in a house filled with German officers. One day, she was fixing her radio antenna to a tree outside her window so she could start sending her messages. A German officer asked her what she was doing. Inayat Khan told him it was a clothesline, and he helped her fix it in place. She then hung her washing on it. When the washing was dry, Inayat Khan sent her radio messages.

Princess Noor Inayat Khan.

Late for school

Inayat Khan sent radio messages almost every day. She collected these messages from a school outside Paris. One day she was late getting there. As she came down the road on her bicycle, she saw German soldiers enter the school building. Inayat Khan hid behind a hedge and watched as the other agents were forced into a truck and driven away. Inayat Khan hurried back to Paris and radioed a message about the raid.

Warned to flee

The British told Inayat Khan to leave France at once, but she stayed on. She was the only radio operator left in her area, and felt it was her duty to stay. One afternoon, Inayat Khan came home to find a German agent searching her room. She tried to get away. The man had to call for help because she put up a strong fight.

Inayat Khan was taken to German headquarters. Within an hour, she tried to escape by climbing out of a bathroom window and onto a ledge five storys up. Guards spotted her, and she was forced to climb back in. When the Germans questioned her, Inayat Khan could not tell a lie. She admitted that she was a spy but she told them nothing else. She was sent to a German prison. Some time after September 13, 1944, she was executed.

The type of suitcase radio used by Inayat Khan.

headquarters   a central place where information is sent and plans are made

Sufi   an Eastern religion

TAKEO YOSHIKAWA, JAPAN'S PEARL HARBOR SPY

BACKGROUND

- For the first two years of World War II, the U.S. did not send soldiers to fight.

- The U.S. finally joined the war after Japan attacked its naval base at Pearl Harbor.

The spy, Takeo Yoshikawa.

Yoshikawa's spy mission

Takeo Yoshikawa was a Japanese naval officer who came to Honolulu in March 1941. He used the cover name Tadasi Morimura and pretended to work for the Japanese embassy. Yoshikawa's real job was to gather information about U.S. warships in Pearl Harbor. To pay for this mission, Yoshikawa was given six new $100 bills.

Picnics and afternoon tea

To get the information he needed, Yoshikawa went on picnics. Sometimes he spent whole days sitting on a hilltop, watching the warships come and go. He often had meals at a Japanese tea-house that overlooked Pearl Harbor. From the windows, he could count the number of sailors on each U.S. ship. He also watched U.S. patrol planes take off each morning. He noted where the planes flew to and what time they returned. Yoshikawa noticed that the patrol planes hardly ever flew out over the ocean to the north of Oahu Island.

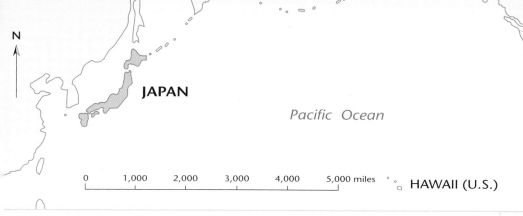

JAPAN

Pacific Ocean

UNITED STATES
OF AMERICA

0   1,000   2,000   3,000   4,000   5,000 miles

HAWAII (U.S.)

German friends

Yoshikawa was helped by a German family named Kühn. Mrs Kühn had a hairdressing shop where wives of U.S. naval officers came to have their hair done. Mrs Kühn listened for any details the wives might let slip about the U.S. fleet. Ruth Kühn, her daughter, dated young American officers. She got them to tell her when any of the ships were getting ready to leave. Mr Kühn sent this information to Yoshikawa across the bay. He used a code of flashing lights signaled from the attic window of his house.

The big day

Yoshikawa had watched U.S. warships come and go for nine months. He was able to tell the Japanese navy that most of the ships stayed in Pearl Harbor on Sundays. Yoshikawa sent his last message one Saturday evening. Next morning, December 7, 1941, Japanese bombers appeared in the sky north of Oahu Island. Wave after wave of them attacked the U.S. ships, sinking five of the battleships in 30 minutes. Nine other warships were badly damaged and more than 2,300 sailors were killed.

Escape

The Kühns were caught at their attic window sending signals even while the attack took place. They were sent to prison for the rest of the war. Yoshikawa escaped back to Japan and was given a medal.

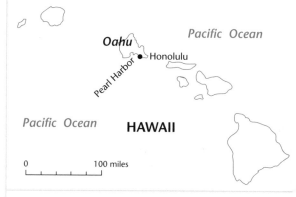

Pacific Ocean

Oahu
Pearl Harbor • Honolulu

Pacific Ocean   **HAWAII**

0   100 miles

The warship USS *Shaw* explodes during the Japanese attack on Pearl Harbor.

cover name   a false name used to hide a spy's true identity

embassy   a building where officials from another country work and sometimes live

ELYESA BAZNA, CODE NAME CICERO

Elyesa Bazna, also known as Cicero.

Elyesa Bazna: 1905–71
Born: Pristina, Yugoslavia (a province of Turkey at that time)
Spied for Germany against Britain

The black box

In 1943, Elyesa Bazna became the personal servant of the British ambassador in Ankara. He looked after the ambassador's clothes, filled his bath, and woke him each morning with a glass of orange juice. The ambassador brought home secret papers every evening, which he would read before going to sleep. The papers were kept in a black box on his bedside table. This box was always locked. One morning when the ambassador went to have his bath, he left the key on the bedside table. Bazna had been waiting for this moment. He pressed the key into a piece of wax and used this wax to have a copy of the key made.

Unlocking the box

Bazna unlocked the black box whenever he got the chance. He removed the papers and hid them inside his coat. He took the papers to his room and photographed the pages one by one using an ordinary Leica camera. He then returned the papers to the box and locked it.

In the shadows

Bazna sent a note to the German embassy saying that he had documents for sale. He received a note back asking him to meet an agent in the shadows behind the embassy building. When the agent arrived, he showed Bazna £20,000 in English notes. This would be Bazna's payment if the documents he was offering were any good. The German agent took the roll of film and left Bazna waiting in the dark. Bazna began to think he had walked into a trap. Fifteen minutes later, the German agent returned and handed over the money. "Until tomorrow," the agent said. He wanted to buy more.

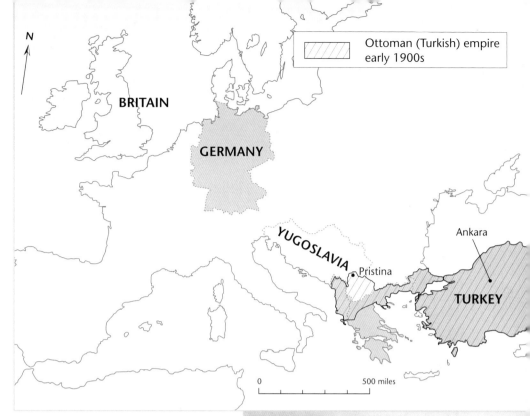

Code name Cicero

Bazna was given the code name Cicero. For the next six months, he unlocked the British ambassador's box and photographed the pages it contained. Bazna had no idea what he was stealing. He handed over some of the biggest secrets of the war. One of the pages he photographed showed details of a British plan to invade Europe. This document was so important and secret that the Germans did not believe it was real until the invasion began.

A Leica camera. Bazna used a similar camera to photograph the secret papers.

The end of Bazna's career

In 1944, a woman working in the German embassy fell in love with a U.S. agent. She told this agent who Cicero was. Bazna had just enough time to pack his bags and flee Ankara. He took with him all the money the Germans had paid him—£300,000. However, when he tried to spend it, Bazna found that most of the money was counterfeit (not real).

ambassador a person who officially represents a country

code name a simple name used to hide the identity of a spy

hotbed a place where things grow rapidly

MATHILDE CARRÉ, THE SPY WHO TURNED TRAITOR

Mathilde Carré: 1908–70
Born: Paris, France
Spied for France against Germany; for Germany against France; and for Britain against Germany

BACKGROUND

When Germany invaded France in 1940, ordinary French people set up secret networks known as the Underground.

The Underground in Paris was called Interallié, or the Allied Circle.

The party girl joins the Underground

Mathilde Carré liked to enjoy herself and often went to parties. All this stopped when Paris fell to the Germans. Soldiers filled the streets, and the French people were scared. Carré hated the war because she could not have a good time any more.

Then, in 1940, she fell in love with a handsome Polish pilot. His name was Captain Czeriavski, and he was the leader of the Interallié in Paris. Carré asked to join him in his work. She learned to use invisible ink and send radio messages in code.

Captured by the Germans

In November 1941, German police raided the Interallié headquarters. Carré and Captain Czeriavski were taken away and questioned. Czeriavski was tortured. The Germans knew the best way to get information out of Carré. One of their officers took her to a Paris restaurant and ordered a fine meal. He told Carré that she had two choices. She could spy for the Germans and live a life of luxury, or she could be shot.

Carré becomes a traitor

Carré became a double agent. She pretended to work for the French, while she really worked for the Germans. She set up meetings with Interallié agents in cafés. Once the agents arrived, Carré would go to the bathroom and German soldiers would swoop. She had 100 Interallié agents arrested this way.

Carré fools the British

Carré kept sending false messages to Britain in secret code. One time, the British sent a special agent across into France to work with the Interallié group. Carré was the only member the agent met. He thought Interallié was very well run and very secret. He asked Carré to return to Britain with him so she could help the Interallié group there. Carré's German spy chief told her to go. He wanted her to spy on the British from right inside their secret-service headquarters.

Carré becomes a triple agent

On the night of February 26, 1942, a British torpedo boat picked up Carré from a French beach. By this time, the British agent had become suspicious of her. As soon as they were out at sea, he accused her of working for the Germans. Carré burst into tears and told him everything. She offered to become a triple agent and work for the British by sending false information back to the Germans. The British let her do this for two months, and then they put her in prison. They felt that Carré could not be trusted. She was returned to France to stand trial after the war.

Hitler and his German generals in Paris after Germany invaded France.

Mathilde Carré. After the war ended, a French court sentenced her to life in prison.

triple agent   a spy who works for three different countries

DONALD KENNEDY, THE COAST WATCHER

BACKGROUND

In World War II, Japan planned to conquer the whole of the South Pacific, including Australia.

Spies known as "coast watchers" went to tiny islands across Australia's north. From there they radioed back reports about the Japanese.

Donald Kennedy: 1916–
Born: New Zealand
Spied for the Allies against Japan

Kennedy sets up a secret base

In 1941, Captain Donald Kennedy of the Royal Australian Navy landed on tiny Segi Island in the Solomon Islands group. He set up a secret spy base in an empty plantation house. Thousands of Japanese soldiers were camped on the islands around him. Kennedy watched them come and go. Every day, he sent radio messages to Australia about the movement of Japanese ships, troops, and planes. Each message was sent in code and had to be very short. Long messages could be traced back to their source.

The secret army

Kennedy soon persuaded the local Solomon Islands people to help him. About 70 local men formed a group they called Kennedy's army. Kennedy trained these men as soldiers, and they often went on spy missions for him. They helped Kennedy move around the island and remain hidden from the Japanese. They also set up a "forbidden zone" around his plantation house, and captured or shot any Japanese entering this zone.

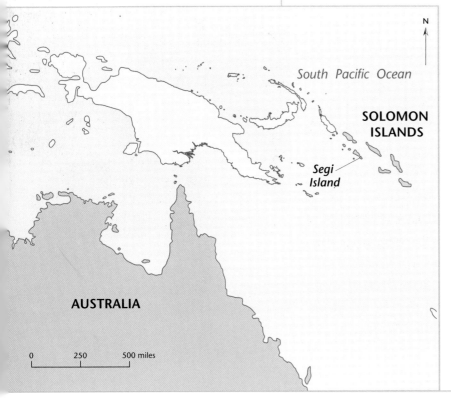

South Pacific Ocean

SOLOMON ISLANDS

Segi Island

AUSTRALIA

0   250   500 miles

Kennedy's navy

One time, Kennedy's army of islanders found a damaged barge left behind by the Japanese. They towed it behind their canoes into a hidden bay. There they repaired the barge. It was ready to put to sea a week later. The next boat that Kennedy's soldiers took from the Japanese was a large sailing ship, with machine guns on its decks. Kennedy's navy was ready for action.

A sea battle

In April 1943, a Japanese troop boat started searching the bays of Segi Island. The Japanese knew that Kennedy was there somewhere. Kennedy had two choices. He could hide or he could attack. Kennedy put to sea in the sailing ship. His islander helpers launched their war canoes. Together they made for the Japanese troop ship and ran it down.

His own P.O.W. camp

Kennedy lived on Segi Island for two years, hiding and sending radio messages. During this time, he saved the lives of 28 U.S. pilots shot down over the sea. He also saved a number of Japanese pilots shot down. He kept these Japanese pilots in a small prisoner-of-war (P.O.W.) camp built by the Solomon Islanders. It was hidden deep inside the "forbidden zone." The islanders guarded this P.O.W. camp 24 hours a day. When the war ended, Britain and the U.S. awarded Donald Kennedy medals for bravery and distinguished (extra special) service.

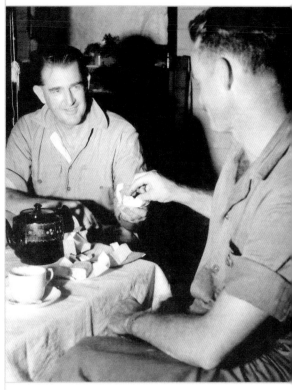

Donald Kennedy having tea with a U.S. intelligence officer in his plantation house on Segi Island.

Kennedy and his native soldiers bring a blindfolded Japanese prisoner into the "forbidden zone."

barge   a motor boat with a wide, flat deck

plantation   a large, tropical farm

CHRISTINE GRANVILLE, BEAUTY QUEEN AND SPY

BACKGROUND

- Germany invaded Poland in 1939 and defeated the Polish army.

- Polish soldiers trying to escape needed help to get away through neighboring European countries.

Countess Krystyna Skarbek, also known as Christine Granville: 1915–52
Born: Warsaw, Poland
Spied for Poland, Britain, and France against Germany

Beauty queen

Krystyna Skarbek was a pretty girl from a rich Polish family. At the age of 17, she won the Miss Poland Beauty Contest. When her country was invaded by Germany, she went to England and trained as a spy. There she took the false name Christine Granville and returned to Europe to work under cover as a journalist in Budapest. Secretly she made many journeys back and forth across the borders of Poland, Czechoslovakia, Hungary, and Yugoslavia, helping soldiers and refugees escape.

Daring escapes

One time, Granville skied across the Tatra Mountains into Poland to bring out a small group of wounded prisoners-of-war. Another time, she was driving four English pilots from Yugoslavia to Hungary. They were stopped by German border guards. Granville told the guards that she and her friends were on a picnic. She invited the guards along, and even offered to open her backpack and give them a beer. German soldiers were forbidden to drink with the local people. They told her to move on. She then asked them to push her car because it had stalled.

Countess Skarbek, who spied under the false name Christine Granville.

Fooling the Germans

Granville was delivering secret documents one day when she spotted a German patrol on the road ahead. She threw the documents into the river. However, she was still carrying a large sum of money when the guards searched her. This made the guards suspicious. Granville told them boldly that they could shoot her and give the money to their commander. Or they could keep the money themselves and let her go. They pocketed the money and let her escape.

Threatening the French

Granville was forced to leave Hungary when the German secret police became suspicious of her. She went to France to work with the Resistance fighters there. The leader of her Resistance group was captured, along with an English spy and a U.S. spy. All three men were taken to a German prison being run by French collaborators. Granville marched into the prison and told the two Frenchmen in charge that U.S. troops had already landed in France. The war would be over in a few days, she declared. She also told them that all French collaborators would be hung if they did not change sides now. The frightened Frenchmen handed over the three spies. Granville bundled them into a car and drove them to safety.

Killed by a madman

Christine Granville died soon after the war. She was murdered by a stranger who had fallen madly in love with her.

The Tatra Mountains.

collaborators   people who help their country's enemy

journalist   a person who writes news stories

refugees   people seeking safety in another country

under cover   pretending to be someone else

TED HALL, THE BOY WHO GAVE AWAY THE ATOM BOMB

BACKGROUND

Towards the end of World War II, several U.S. scientists developed a new super weapon called the atom bomb.

This bomb was meant to end the war.

It was also meant to prevent wars by making other countries too afraid to go to war again.

Ted Hall: 1925–99
Born: New York, U.S. (of Russian parents)
Spied for the Soviet Union against the U.S.

The whiz kid

Ted Hall was a gifted child. At school, he moved quickly from grade to grade. By the age of 16, he was studying physics at Harvard University, in Cambridge. At 18, Hall was asked if he would work on a secret weapons project in an isolated laboratory in Los Alamos. Hall was told that this project would end the war. He went to Los Alamos and found himself working on the atom bomb.

Implosion!

Many scientists worked at Los Alamos trying to build the bomb. A special explosion was needed at the bomb's center to set off the powerful nuclear blast. Hall discovered the sort of explosion needed—an implosion! This occurs when the core explodes inwards on itself. However, Hall was worried as he worked on the bomb. He did not like the idea of only one country in the world having such a super weapon. He believed this would give that country too much power.

Ted Hall, aged 16.

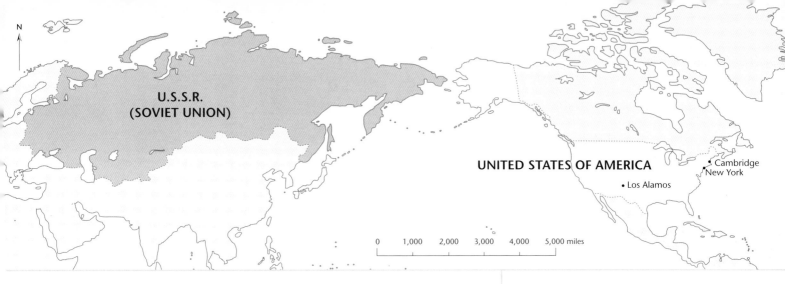

U.S.S.R.
(SOVIET UNION)

UNITED STATES OF AMERICA
• Cambridge
New York
• Los Alamos

0   1,000   2,000   3,000   4,000   5,000 miles

Playing the game of spies

Hall talked to his friend Saville Sax about his fears. Together the two young men came up with a plan to help another country build an atom bomb as well. The Soviet Union was the country they chose. It was the only other country in the world with enough money and scientists to do the job.

Hall went to the office of a Soviet trading company in New York. There he found a man stacking boxes and told him that he had important information to give away about atomic experiments. The Soviets were interested. Two months later, Sax became Hall's courier and met with a Soviet agent. Sax gave the man two pieces of paper he had hidden in his shoe. On these pages, in Hall's own handwriting, were details of how an atom bomb might work. Over the next few years, Sax handed over many more atomic secrets supplied by Hall.

The first atom bomb. It was dropped on Japan on August 6, 1945.

The round-up

When the Soviets exploded their first atom bomb in 1949, the U.S. knew someone had given its secrets away. All the atomic scientists were investigated. Other scientists had also given away atomic secrets, and two were arrested. No evidence was found against Hall and he carried on working as a scientist for the rest of his life. In 1995, Hall's name showed up on some old, secret Soviet files. At last he admitted that he had been a spy. It was too late to send Hall to jail as he was then 70 years old.

Soviet Union   a shortened name for the Union of Soviet Socialist Republics (U.S.S.R.), once called Russia

HANS AND SOPHIE SCHOLL, AND THE *WHITE ROSE*

Hans Scholl: 1918–43
Sophie Scholl: 1921–43
Born: Forchtenberg, Germany
Spied against the Nazis

BACKGROUND

- In 1933, Adolf Hitler and his Nazi Party promised to make life better for the German people.

- Once Hitler came to power, he started doing terrible things.

Hans (left) and Sophie Scholl with a friend.

articles   essays and stories for newspapers

resist   to stand against

Students at Munich University

In 1942, Hans and Sophie Scholl were students at Munich University. At this time, Hitler's secret police arrested anyone who did not agree with the Nazis. These people were often executed and their families imprisoned. Hans Scholl and his university friends wanted to do something about this. They began printing a one-page newspaper called the *White Rose*. In this newspaper, they wrote articles asking the German people to resist the Nazis in peaceful ways.

Sophie and Hans work together

Sophie soon joined her brother in this work. They mailed copies of the *White Rose* to important people, such as doctors and university teachers. On February 18, 1943, Sophie and Hans took their *White Rose* leaflets to the university and scattered them along the corridors. All the students were in class, but the university handyman spotted them. Hans and Sophie were arrested by the Nazi police. They were questioned for four days. Neither Hans nor Sophie betrayed their friends. They faced court together and were executed on the same day, February 22, 1943.

GLOSSARY

Allied soldiers   soldiers fighting on the side of the Allies (Britain, Belgium, and France)

ally   a country that helps and supports another country

ambassador   a person who officially represents a country

articles   essays and stories for newspapers

barge   a motor boat with a wide, flat deck

civilian   a person not in the armed forces

code name   a simple name used to hide the identity of a spy

codes   secret languages

collaborators   people who help their country's enemy

convoys   lines of vehicles

cover name   a false name used to hide a spy's true identity

double agent   a spy pretending to work for one country while secretly working for another

embassy   a building where officials from another country work and sometimes live

headquarters   a central place where information is sent and plans are made

hotbed   a place where things grow rapidly

identity card   an official card with a person's name and photograph that proves who they are

into the field   going into other countries to spy

invaded   used military force to enter someone else's land

journalist   a person who writes news stories

license   a document showing that a person has been given permission to do a special task or job

navigator   a person who works out which direction to go

Nazi Party   a brutal political and military group that governed Germany from 1933 to 1949

neutral   not taking one side or the other in a fight

papier-mâché   wet paper and paste that is molded into shape and dries hard

passport   an official identification document needed by someone traveling to another country

plantation   a large, tropical farm

recruited   asked to do a job

refueling stop   a place to fill up with more fuel

refugees   people seeking safety in another country

resist   to stand against

secret service   another name for a spy network

Soviet Union   a shortened name for the Union of Soviet Socialist Republics (U.S.S.R.), once called Russia

Sufi   an Eastern religion

triple agent   a spy who works for three different countries

under cover   pretending to be someone else

INDEX

A
Allies *5–6, 8–9, 13*
ambassador *20–21*
Atlantic Ocean *10*
atom bomb *28–29*
Auschwitz *14–15*
Australia *24*
Axis powers *5*

B
Bazna, Elyesa (Cicero) *20–21*
Britain *5–7, 9, 12, 16, 20, 22–23, 25–26*

C
Canaris, Wilhelm *8–9*
Carré, Mathilde *22–23*
Channel Islands *12*
Chapman, Eddie *12–13*
coast watchers *24*
collaborators *27*
Czechoslovakia *26*
Czeriavski, Captain *22*

D
double agent *13, 23*

E
Earhart, Amelia *10–11*
England *6, 9, 12–13, 16, 26*
Europe *5, 21*

F
France *6–7, 16–17, 22–23, 26–27*

G
Germany *5–6, 8–9, 12, 14, 16, 20–21, 22–23, 26, 30*
Granville, Christine (Krystyna Skarbek) *26–27*

H
Hall, Ted *28–29*
Hitler *5, 8–9, 23, 30*
Hungary *26–27*

I
identity cards *4*
Inayat Khan, Noor *16–17*
intelligence officer *4, 25*
invisible ink *22*
Italy *8*

J
Japan *5, 10, 18–19, 24*
Jews *9*

K
Kennedy, Donald *24–25*

L
Los Alamos *28–29*

N
Nazi *5, 8–9, 30*
New Zealand *6, 24*

P
Pacific Ocean *10–11*
patrol boats *10*
Pearl Harbor *18–19*
Pilecki, Witold *14–15*
Poland *5, 14–15, 26*
prisoner-of-war camp *25*

R
radio antenna *16*
radio codes *16*
radio messages *5, 11, 16–17, 22, 24–25*
radio transmitter *4*
refugees *26*
Resistance fighters *7, 27*
Russia *16*

S
Scholl, Hans and Sophie *30*
secret code *16, 22, 23*
Solomon Islands *24–25*
Soviet Union *28–29*
Spain *6, 8*
spy chief *12, 23*
submarine *8*

T
triple agent *23*
Turkey *20*

U
Underground, the *6, 14–15, 22*
United States *10, 18, 25, 28*

W
Wake, Nancy *6–7*

Y
Yoshikawa, Takeo *18–19*
Yugoslavia *20, 26*